IT'S BEDTIME, LITTLE CRITTER!

BY MERCER MAYER

RANDOM HOUSE 🏠 NEW YORK

Just Go to Bed book, characters, text, and images copyright © 1983 by Mercer Mayer,
and *What a Bad Dream* book, characters, text, and images copyright © 1992 by Mercer Mayer

Little Critter, Mercer Mayer's Little Critter, and Mercer Mayer's Little Critter and Logo
are registered trademarks of Orchard House Licensing Company.

Visit us on the Web! • rhcbooks.com • littlecritter.com
ISBN 978-1-5247-6900-0
Printed in the United States of America
10 9 8 7 6 5 4 3

JUST GO TO BED

BY
MERCER MAYER

I'm a cowboy and
I round up cows.
I can lasso anything.

Dad says . . .

"It's time for the cowboy to come inside and get ready for bed."

I'm a general and I have to stop the enemy army with my tank.

Dad says ...

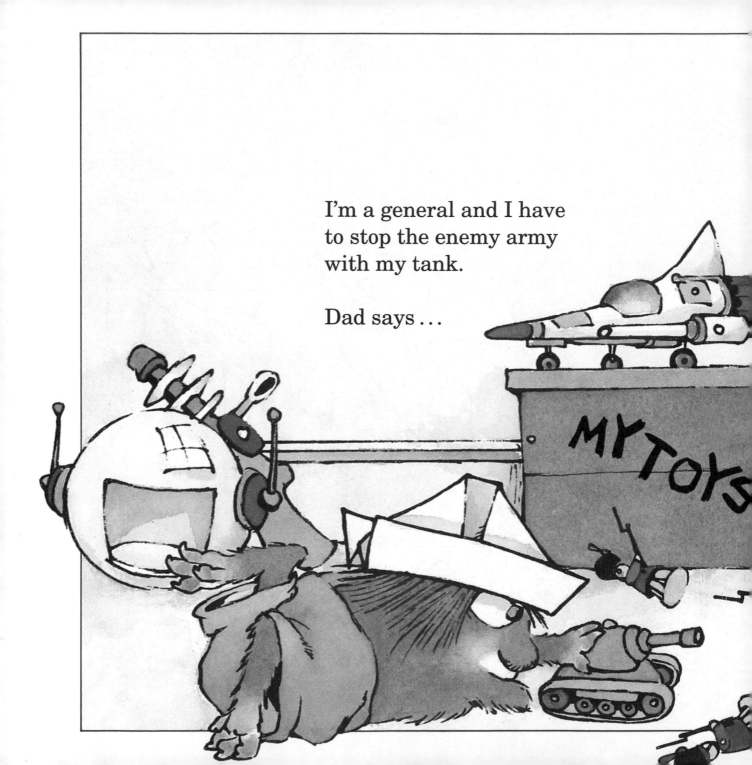

"It's time for the general to take a bath."

I'm a space cadet and I zoom
to the moon.

I capture a robot
with my ray gun.

Dad says . . .

"This giant robot has captured the space cadet and is going to put him in the bathtub right now."

Dad says, "It's time for the sea monster to have a snack."

I'm a zookeeper feeding
my hungry animals.

Dad says ...

"Feeding time is over. Here are
the zookeeper's pajamas."

Dad says,
"The bandit chief
has caught you,
so put on
your pajamas."

But I'm a race car driver
and I just speed away.

Dad says, "The race is over.
Now put on these pajamas
and go to bed."

I'm a bunny hopping
around my garden.

Dad says . . .

"But I'm a bunny and bunnies
don't sleep in a bed."

Mom says, "Shhh!"
Dad says, "Go to sleep."

Well, maybe a tired bunny
could sleep in a bed ...

just this once.

WHAT A BAD DREAM

BY MERCER MAYER

I had a dream that I made a magic potion. After I mixed it up, I drank the potion down.

Then weird things started to happen,
just like in a spooky show on television.

I changed.
I grew pointy fangs

and long claws.

I had bat wings and a long tail.

I could roar so loud that I scared everybody,
and they left me alone.
Then I did whatever I wanted.

I lived all by myself.
My room looked just the way I wanted it to look.

I had cookies and ice cream for breakfast.

I never brushed my fur or my fangs,
and I never changed my clothes.

I got a gorilla for a pet.

I didn't go to school.
I just rode my bicycle
wherever I wanted.

SALE TODAY

We ate ice cream and fudge pops for lunch.

We played outside as long as we wanted—
even after it was dark.

At dinnertime we just
ordered in pizza
and didn't use napkins.

I never took a bath—even if I was dirty.
I kept lizards and frogs and snakes in the tub.

I watched television as late as I wanted and never even had to go to bed.

I got sleepy anyway and went upstairs.
But there was no one to tuck me in
and read me a story.

Then I got scared, and there was no one
to give me a hug. I began to cry.
I wanted my mommy and daddy.

Suddenly someone was shaking me.
It was my mom and dad.
"You had a bad dream," they said.

"Time to put you in bed," said Dad.
"That's not a magic potion, is it?" I asked.

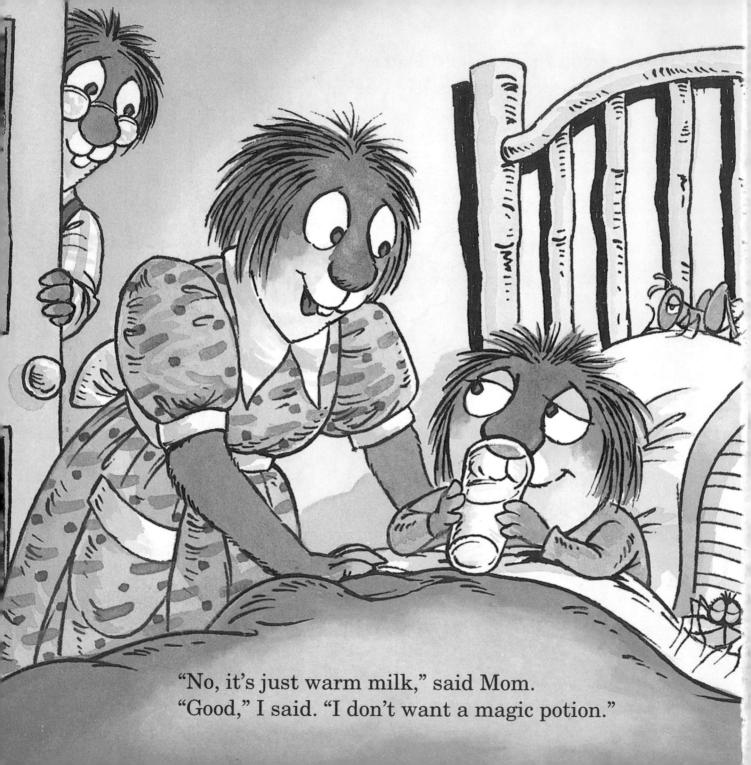

"No, it's just warm milk," said Mom.
"Good," I said. "I don't want a magic potion."